The
Tiniest
Puppy

Pet Rescue Adventures:
Max the Missing Puppy
Ginger the Stray Kitten
Buttons the Runaway Puppy
The Frightened Kitten
Jessie the Lonely Puppy
The Kitten Nobody Wanted
Harry the Homeless Puppy
Lost in the Snow
Leo All Alone
The Brave Kitten
The Secret Puppy
Sky the Unwanted Kitten
Misty the Abandoned Kitten
The Scruffy Puppy
The Lost Puppy
The Missing Kitten
The Secret Kitten
The Rescued Puppy
Sammy the Shy Kitten

Also by Holly Webb:
Little Puppy Lost

The Tiniest Puppy

by Holly Webb
Illustrated by Sophy Williams

tiger tales

For William and Robin

tiger tales

5 River Road, Suite 128, Wilton, CT 06897
Published in the United States 2017
Originally published as *Lucy the Poorly Puppy* in Great Britain 2011
by Little Tiger Press
Text copyright © 2011 Holly Webb
Illustrations copyright © 2011 Sophy Williams
Author photograph copyright © Nigel Bird
My Naughty Little Puppy illustration copyright © Kate Pankhurst
ISBN-13: 978-1-68010-403-5
ISBN-10: 1-68010-403-9
Printed in China
STP/1800/0115/0816
10 9 8 7 6 5 4 3 2 1

For more insight and activities, visit us at www.tigertalesbooks.com

Chapter One

"Baylee looks so big!" Lauren peered under the kitchen table at the family's beagle. They had adopted Baylee from the rescue shelter last year, and she had settled in with the family quite nicely. She was sitting at their feet, panting and looking uncomfortable. Her tummy was huge, and the expression on her face was a little grumpy.

Dad checked under the table, too. "Well, she's due to have the puppies any day now. I'll take her temperature later to see if it has gone down."

Lauren nodded. They had been taking Baylee's temperature every day for the last couple of weeks. The vet, Mike, had told them it was the best way to tell when the puppies were about to come.

Baylee padded heavily out from under the table and wandered over to her cushion. She took hold of the edge in her teeth—it was a big, soft cushion, made of red fabric—and tugged it closer to the radiator. Then she nudged it with her nose, this way and that, as though she couldn't get it quite how she wanted it.

Lauren watched her hopefully. "Does that look like nesting to you?" she asked.

"I don't know. It might be...," her mom said doubtfully. It was the first time Baylee had had puppies, and they were having to learn as they went along, even though Lauren's mom had bought three different books on dog breeding.

"We need to leave for school," Dad

pointed out, checking his watch.

Lauren sighed. "I bet Baylee is going to have the puppies while I'm at school, and I really, really want to be here. Couldn't I just stay home? It's the last day of the semester; we're not going to actually do anything, are we?"

Mom shook her head. "No, you can't stay home. Besides, don't you want to say good-bye to all your friends? You won't see most of them for the next two months, remember."

Lauren frowned. It was true. She loved living way out in the country. Their home had been a farmhouse originally, and it had a huge yard. The old cowsheds had been made into her parents' office, and there was a barn across the yard that Lauren could play in. But there were bad things about it, too. She lived twenty minutes away from the town where her school was, and her best friend, Carolyn, lived in a town that was about twenty minutes beyond the school! So arranging to see Carolyn during vacations always meant a lot of planning.

Lauren grabbed her bag and the present she'd gotten for her teacher, Miss Ford, and took one last look at Baylee on the way out of the kitchen. The beautiful brown and white dog was squirming around on her cushion as though she couldn't quite get comfy.

"Can you just hold on until I get home?" Lauren pleaded. But Baylee looked up at her with big, mournful eyes. Lauren petted her lovingly.

"I see what you mean. You must really want to be back to your old self again. If it happens today, good luck, Baylee. It'll be worth it. You're going to have beautiful puppies soon."

"She's going to be very tired," Dad pointed out. "We'll have to take care of her. I remember doing all this with Rosie, my parents' dog, when I was just a bit older than you. Now come on, Lauren, we're going to be late."

As they were bumping down the side street in the car toward the main road, Lauren asked, "How many puppies do you think Baylee will have?"

Dad shook his head. "Hard to tell—could be anything from one to 14, according to those books your mom bought. Rosie had only five."

Lauren frowned. "It can't just be one. Baylee is enormous."

"I think you're probably right—she is very big. I'd say we're looking at quite a few," Dad agreed.

He sighed as he noted her sparkling eyes and excited smile. "Lauren...."

"What?" Lauren looked over at him worriedly.

"Sweetheart, just remember that we aren't keeping these puppies. They're all going to new homes."

Lauren hesitated for a moment. "I know," she said quietly. She was silent for a little while and then added, "But we'll have them for a couple of months, won't we? That's all of summer vacation to play with them, and more."

Dad nodded. "Exactly. Of course

we'll miss them when they go, but it'll be easier if we remember that they aren't ours to keep."

"I won't forget," Lauren promised. "Oh, there's Carolyn, Dad! Can you let me out here? I can walk up the street to school with her and her mom, can't I?"

Dad pulled up, and Lauren jumped out of the car, waving to her best friend.

"Hi! How's Baylee? Has she had the puppies yet?" Carolyn asked breathlessly.

Lauren shook her head, then smiled. "Baylee was being really funny this morning. She kept messing around with her bed as if she were nesting. There might even be puppies when I get home!" she said, swinging her school bag excitedly.

"You're so lucky," said Carolyn. "Mom, can we have one of Baylee's puppies? Pleeeease?"

"Oh, Carolyn, you know I'd love one," said her mom, hitching Carolyn's baby sister, Amy, higher up on her hip. "But it just wouldn't be fair to have a dog. I'm busy with your sister, and your dad's at work during the day. A puppy would get lonely."

Carolyn sighed. "I suppose so."

"You'll be able to play with them when you come over during vacation," Lauren promised her. "And I won't get to keep the puppies, either. Dad was reminding me in the car."

Carolyn nodded. "Still, you'll have weeks and weeks to play with them all. Oh, there's the bell. See you later, Mom!"

The two girls ran into class, and joined the crowd of children around Miss Ford, all begging her to open their good-bye present first.

Chapter Two

Lauren usually spent a long time chatting with all her friends at the end of school, but today she was desperate to see if the puppies had arrived. She dashed out into the playground to find Dad waiting by the gate. Carolyn chased after her.

"Has Baylee had the puppies yet?" Lauren gasped. She'd been running so fast she had to grab on to Dad's arm to stop herself from falling over.

Dad steadied her, laughing. "Yes."

"How many?" Lauren squeaked excitedly.

Dad smiled. "Guess."

Lauren frowned. "Five?"

"Nowhere near. 10!"

"Wow! 10 puppies?" Lauren turned around to Carolyn, her eyes round with amazement. "10? That's a *huge* litter!"

Carolyn laughed. "You'll have to think of 10 names!"

"That's going to be tricky," Dad said. Lauren gave him a worried look. He didn't sound quite as happy as she thought the owner of 10 puppies should. A sudden horrible thought hit her. Ten puppies was a lot—it must have been such hard work for Baylee, giving birth to so many. What if something was wrong with her? Lauren opened her mouth to ask, and then shut it again. She didn't want to talk about something so scary in the middle of the school playground.

Instead, she hugged Carolyn good-bye and promised to email her a picture of the puppies later.

But as soon as she and Dad were heading for the car, she grabbed his hand. "Dad, is everything okay?"

"What do you mean?" Dad looked at her carefully.

"I just thought you seemed a little worried—after you told us there were so many puppies. Is Baylee all right?"

Dad gave her a hug. "Baylee's fine. I mean, she's exhausted, but she did really well. It's not Baylee...." He hesitated. "Lauren, one of the puppies is a lot smaller than the others. Mom and I—we're not sure this one will make it. It's such a tiny little thing, and when it was first born, we weren't even sure if it was breathing. Baylee had another puppy right after, and she didn't have time to lick the little puppy like she did with the others, or bite through its cord. I had to cut the cord myself, and I rubbed the puppy with a blanket to bring it around." He shook his head. "It did start to breathe, but it's not as strong as the other puppies, not by a long shot. It's just so tiny."

"Do you think it might die, Dad?" Lauren whispered.

Dad sighed. "I hope not—but we have to face the fact that it might."

"That's so sad." Lauren felt tears stinging her eyes. The poor little puppy.

"Nine healthy puppies is a great litter," Dad reminded her.

Lauren nodded. "I guess so. But I can't help worrying about the little one."

"I know. Me, too. Still, it might perk up. You never know."

Lauren crossed her fingers behind her back. She wanted Baylee to have all 10 of her wonderful puppies safe and well.

Lauren crept in the kitchen door. She was trying very hard not to upset Baylee.

But Baylee looked like she'd be impossible to disturb. She was stretched flat out on her side, fast asleep on the pile of old towels that Mom had put aside for her and the puppies to sleep on, in the special low wooden pen that Dad had made for them. They'd been worried that the puppies might fall off of Baylee's big cushion.

The puppies were all snuggled up next to their mom, fast asleep in a pile of heads and paws. Lauren knelt down beside the pen and tried to count them, but she couldn't figure out where one puppy ended and the next began.

She couldn't see which was the one that Dad was worried about, either.

"They're so tiny!" she whispered to Mom.

"I know, aren't they beautiful?" Mom beamed.

Lauren frowned. "They're all black-and-white! I can hardly see any brown on them at all. That's really weird, considering that Baylee is brown and white."

Mom shook her head. "I thought that, but then I looked it up in our beagle book, and it says they're usually born mostly black-and-white. The black might change to brown during the next few weeks, or stay as it is. Most beagles are black-and-white with brown patches—tricolor, it's called. Baylee's pretty rare, all brown and white."

"Look how pink their noses are," Lauren breathed. "And I can hear them snuffling! They're so adorable."

"Aren't they?" Dad agreed. "Oh, look, Baylee's waking up."

Lauren watched Baylee yawn and blink sleepily, and crouched closer to the pen, expecting Baylee to want to lick her hand. She was such a friendly dog, and she loved to cuddle up with Lauren—especially on the couch watching cartoons.

But today Baylee didn't seem to see her. She was only interested in her puppies. She nudged them awake, pushing them gently toward her tummy so they could start feeding.

"She was like that with me, too," Mom said. "Not interested. It's as if she only has eyes for her puppies now." She put her arm around Lauren's shoulders. "Don't worry. She'll only be like this for the first couple of weeks, until they open their eyes and start to move around. Then they won't need her so much, and she'll be our sweet Baylee again."

Lauren nodded. "Can I pick up one of the puppies?" she asked.

"We haven't touched them yet," Dad said. "We didn't want to upset Baylee."

Lauren peered at the pile of puppies, as Baylee woke them up. "Which is the little one—the one that was having trouble breathing?" she asked anxiously. "Oh! I think I can see—is it the one Baylee's licking?"

Mom nodded. "Yes, that one's definitely a lot smaller than the others."

"Oh, look, you can see its little brown eyebrows!" Lauren said admiringly.

She edged closer to the pen, and Baylee glanced up, as if to check that she wasn't going to harm the puppies. Lauren shuffled back a little, and Baylee quickly went back to licking and nudging at the tiny puppy. The others were all feeding already—Lauren could hear the strange, wheezy squeak as they sucked. She giggled. "Look, Mom, that puppy is sitting on the other one's head!"

Mom smiled. "I don't think they mind as long as they're getting their mom's milk."

Dad was looking at one of the others. "Hey, puppy, I don't think that's going to do you much good," he chuckled. "Look, that big puppy is trying to suck Baylee's paw."

Baylee looked around at the sound of Dad's voice, and spotted the confused puppy. She wrinkled her nose, and then gently pushed the puppy over to her tummy to feed with its brothers and sisters. Then she went back to trying to rouse the tiny puppy.

"That one really is a lot smaller than the others," Lauren said worriedly.

"And it's going to stay that way if it doesn't eat," Dad put in. "Oh, hang on, though. Look. Baylee got it moving."

The littlest puppy scrambled wearily, its paws waving. It was making sad squeaking sounds, as though it wished Baylee had left it to sleep, but at last it managed to burrow in among the rest of the litter.

"Is it feeding?" Mom asked hopefully.

"I think so." Lauren tried to listen for sucking sounds, but it was hard to tell with nine other puppies feeding at the same time. "Its head is moving back and forth, like the others."

Dad nodded. "That's good. I was getting worried."

Then Lauren winced as one of the other puppies kicked the tiny one in the stomach—not on purpose; the bigger puppy was just scrambling to get back to Baylee's milk. The tiny puppy lay there, kicking feebly, and then it seemed to go back to sleep. Lauren watched anxiously, willing it to wake up and feed again. But the littlest puppy just lay where it was, while its brothers and sisters wriggled and kicked for the best spot.

Chapter Three

Hi Carolyn,

Here's a photo of the newborn puppies! I bet you can't count all 10 in this picture, though, since they're all squeezed in together. They're really beautiful, but there's one tiny one that won't feed from Baylee. I just hope it's going to get better. Please come and see the puppies soon.

Love Lauren x

Lauren sent her email to Carolyn, and went downstairs to find Dad making dinner and Mom cuddling one of the puppies, while Baylee sat at the edge of the pen and kept a close eye on her.

"Oh, wow, she let you pick one up!"

Mom nodded. "But I was very careful. I washed my hands, and then I petted Baylee first, so that I didn't make the puppy smell like me. The book I was reading said that it was good to start handling puppies early, to get them used to people, but I don't want to worry Baylee. She doesn't seem too bothered, though—we thought she would be okay, since she's such a friendly dog." Mom ran her finger very gently down the snoozing puppy's back. "If you wash your hands, you can pet the puppy, too."

Lauren carefully washed her hands, and gave Baylee lots of attention first, petting her with both hands to get Baylee's scent on her fingers. Then she petted the puppy with one finger, like her mom had done. It felt like slightly damp velvet—and it was no bigger than one of the beanbag toy dogs she had on her windowsill upstairs. "It's so soft...," she breathed.

Baylee made a little snorting noise, and lay down next to her puppies again, but she was still eyeing Lauren and her mom.

"Look how fat its tummy is," Mom pointed out. "This puppy is absolutely stuffed."

"I think we should put it back," Lauren said. "Baylee looks a little worried. But she hasn't growled or anything. She's such a good dog."

"And a good mother, too," Dad said from the stove. "She's taken to it so well."

Lauren's mom gently slipped the puppy back into the pen next to Baylee, who licked it all over. The puppy made a squeaking noise as Baylee's big tongue licked its head, but it didn't wake up.

"Where's the tiny one?" Lauren asked, trying to count the puppies.

Mom frowned. "I'm sure I saw it just a moment ago, and I think it had some more milk, which is really good. Apparently Baylee's milk is full of all sorts of good stuff on the day they're born. The puppies get all the benefit of the vaccinations she's had, that kind of thing."

"I can't see the little puppy now," Lauren muttered anxiously. "What if it's under all the others and they squash it?"

Mom knelt down next to her. "Isn't that it?" she asked, pointing to a puppy.

Lauren shook her head. "No, brown eyebrows, remember? That one's just black-and-white."

"Oh, yes." Mom edged around to the

other side of the pen. "It's here, behind Baylee. It must have gotten pushed out of the way by the others."

Lauren followed her, moving slowly so as not to disturb Baylee. "Is it okay?"

Baylee was watching carefully, and as soon as she realized what had happened, she wriggled around and tried to nudge the puppy over with her nose. But the puppy was fast asleep and didn't move. Baylee glanced up at Lauren and her mom, almost as though she wasn't quite sure what to do.

"Should we move the puppy for her?" Lauren asked, frowning.

Mom was starting to say, "Maybe we should…," when Baylee leaned down and picked up the tiny puppy in her mouth.

"Mom, what's Baylee doing?" Lauren whispered in horror.

"Don't worry," Mom soothed her. "It's fine. Dogs do that, Lauren; she won't hurt the puppy."

But it didn't look at all comfortable. The puppy's legs dangled out on either side of Baylee's mouth, and it wheezed and squeaked unhappily. Baylee swiftly tucked it next to her tummy and watched hopefully.

Lauren and Mom watched, too, and Dad left the pasta sauce he was stirring and came to peer over their shoulders, holding a wooden spoon covered in tomato sauce.

"It's feeding," Lauren whispered excitedly, seeing the little shoulders moving.

Mom nodded. "And since all the others are asleep, hopefully it'll be able to keep feeding for a while."

"Oh, that's good." Dad sighed with relief. "And good timing. Dinner is ready."

Lauren went to bed that night very reluctantly. She wanted to stay and watch the puppies, especially the tiniest one. She was still worried that it wasn't getting enough milk. Because it wasn't as big as the others, it couldn't wriggle its way back to Baylee when it got pushed away, like the others could. Instead of barging past its brothers and sisters, the littlest puppy would just whine miserably and go back to sleep.

"Can't I stay up a little longer? It's the first day of vacation tomorrow," Lauren begged.

"It's already an hour past bedtime!" Mom pointed out. "You can come down early in the morning to see them. But now you need to go to bed."

Lauren sighed, recognizing Mom's no-argument voice. Still, she was sure she wouldn't ever sleep.

Lauren woke up suddenly to find her bedroom in darkness. So she *had* fallen asleep after all.

She sat up, hugging her knees. What time was it? It felt like the middle of the night. She glanced at her luminous clock. Two o'clock in the morning. Lauren shuddered. No wonder it was so dark. She lay down again, but she didn't feel sleepy anymore. Something was worrying her, and she wasn't sure what it was. Then she realized—the puppies! Of course! How could she have forgotten about them?

She couldn't hear any noise from downstairs. Baylee and the puppies were probably fast asleep. But she couldn't stop worrying that something was wrong, and that was why she had woken up.

It wouldn't hurt to go and take a look, would it? Lauren smiled to herself—Mom had said she could come down early to see the puppies, after all. She probably hadn't meant quite this early, but still....

She got out of bed and crept over to her door, quickly pulling on her robe. As she ran across the landing to the stairs, she could hear her dad snoring. She hurried down the stairs and into the kitchen. She could hear little squeaks and sucking noises—the puppies were awake and feeding, but that wasn't really surprising. Lauren had been reading Mom's puppy books, and it said that for the first couple of weeks, they would need to feed every two hours.

Mom had left a small lamp from the living room plugged in on the counter so Baylee had some light for feeding the puppies. Baylee was lying on her side looking sleepy, but she thumped her tail gently on the floor of the pen when she saw Lauren.

"Hey, Baylee. I just came to see how you all are," Lauren whispered, kneeling beside the pen.

Baylee closed her eyes wearily, as Lauren patted her head and leaned over to count the puppies. Then she counted them again. Only nine!

Where was the little puppy with the brown eyebrows?

"Oh, Baylee, where is it?" Lauren whispered, but Baylee was half-asleep, and she only twitched her tail.

Lauren checked behind Baylee, where the puppy had ended up before, but there was nothing there. She was sure the other puppies weren't lying on the little one, and it couldn't possibly have climbed out. Frantically, Lauren started to feel around the shadowy edges of the box.

"Oh!" Lauren gasped, as she touched something little and soft, pushed away in the corner. "There you are!" She picked up the puppy, waiting for it to squeak and complain, but it didn't make a sound. "Oh, no, I didn't wash my hands—I suppose it's too late now." Lauren lifted the puppy up to see better, and realized that it was saggy and cold in her hands.

"Oh, no, please…," she muttered, and snuggled the puppy in a fold of her robe. "Mom! Dad!" she yelled, as she raced back up the stairs. "We need to call the vet!"

Chapter Four

"It woke up a little bit while I was holding it," Lauren explained to Mike, the vet. "Is it going to be all right?"

Mike put away his stethoscope and looked at the puppy thoughtfully. "You did really well to catch her when you did, Lauren. She's a she, by the way."

Lauren smiled, just a little. She had thought the puppy was a she—it was something about those cute brown eyebrows.

"It looks to me like she was slipping away," Mike went on, gently petting the puppy's head. "Puppies can't control how warm or cold they are; they need their mom to keep them warm. You cuddling her warmed her up again. The real problem is that she's not strong enough to feed properly by herself. But you could hand-rear her." He glanced up at Lauren, and her mom and dad. "I can't promise she'll make it. But it's worth a try. It's a lot of work, though."

Lauren's dad frowned. "What does hand-rearing mean, exactly? I've taken care of puppies before, but I've never had to hand-rear one. Would we feed her with a bottle?"

"A baby's bottle?" Lauren asked, looking at the tiny puppy. She was about the same size as a baby's bottle!

Mike shook his head. "No, a special puppy one. I've got one somewhere." He searched around in the drawer next to him. "Here it is, and here's some puppy milk replacement, and some information on hand-rearing." He handed Lauren's dad a jar of white powder and a pamphlet. "You mix it with water, just like baby formula. Puppies can't drink cows' milk; it has the wrong mix of nutrients for them."

Lauren's dad read the instructions on the jar. "Every two hours?" he asked, sounding slightly worried.

"Only for the first week," Mike reassured him. "After that you'll probably be able to leave her without a feeding through the middle of the night."

Dad rubbed his eyes wearily—it was now four o'clock in the morning. He and Mom ran their own mail-order business from home, and he'd been up late checking orders. He nodded. "Well, that's what we'll do." He glanced at Mom, who was looking anxious. "We can't not," he added gently.

Mom nodded. "Of course. It's going to be hard, though." She smiled at Lauren. "A little bit like when you were little."

Mike smiled. "But puppies grow faster than babies. They stop drinking their mom's milk at about seven weeks old. This little one should be feeding herself before you know it."

Lauren nodded. If it worked…. Mike hadn't sounded absolutely sure that it would. But Lauren had already saved this puppy once, and if she had anything to do with it, the little one was going to make it.

"I'll do it," she said to her parents. "The feeding, I mean. I don't mind."

"You can't get up every two hours in the middle of the night!" Mom said, sounding horrified.

"I can, Mom, please let me!" She looked toward Mike. "We should feed her now, shouldn't we? Do we have to use boiling water? Like Carolyn's mom uses for her little sister's bottles?"

Mike grinned at Lauren's parents. "It sounds like Lauren knows what she's doing."

Lauren beamed at him. She really wanted to help, but she had a feeling Mom and Dad weren't going to want her to do it. "Do we have to keep the puppy separate from the others?" she asked, trying hard to think of anything else they might need to know.

Mike frowned. "I would for tonight. She's obviously having trouble keeping warm, so she'll need a box and a hot-water bottle. The pamphlet shows you.

But after tonight, she'd be better off staying with her mom and the rest of the puppies, if she can. Just take her out for her feedings. Good luck! And if there are any problems, give us a call here at the animal hospital."

As soon as they got back home, Lauren ran to fill the kettle. The boiling water took forever to cool down, and Lauren kept wanting to blow on it.

Mom went to prepare a box for the puppy, and Dad sat at the kitchen table reading the pamphlet that Mike had given them. "Small cardboard box. Blanket. Hot-water bottle," he muttered. "We should have thought about all of this before, but it just never crossed my mind that we'd have so many puppies and Baylee wouldn't be able to feed them all. Ugh!"

"What?" Lauren turned around, still cradling the puppy.

Dad was making a face. "According to this, we're going to have to help the puppy poop, too. They don't do it themselves, apparently, and because Baylee won't be licking her after she's eaten, we'll have to wipe her bottom with wet cotton."

Lauren made a face back. That *was* a bit yucky. But it didn't turn her off. She was going to do everything necessary to keep the puppy going. Even if that meant making her poop.

"I think this water is cool enough to

mix the formula now. Not long until you can have some milk, Bitsy."

"Bitsy?" Mom asked. "When did you name her?"

Lauren looked up. "I didn't even notice I had! But don't you think she looks like a Bitsy?"

Mom nodded, but she was frowning, and Lauren bit her lip. She had a horrible feeling that Mom hadn't wanted her to name the tiny puppy in case she didn't make it.

Lauren carefully spooned the powder into the bottle, and mixed in the water. "Wake up, little one…. Does it say how to hold her, Dad?"

Her dad skimmed through the instructions. "Flat, on her tummy, not on her back like a human baby. Here, look, on a towel." He laid a towel over Lauren's knees, and Lauren set Bitsy down on her tummy. Her paws splayed out and she scratched a little and let out a tiny squeak, unsure of what was going on.

"It's okay." Lauren picked up the bottle and gently put it against Bitsy's mouth.

"Squeeze the bottle a little," Mom suggested. "She doesn't know what it is. Let her taste a few drops of the milk."

All of a sudden Bitsy started to suck eagerly, as she tasted the milk in her mouth. Her tiny pink paws, with their little transparent claws, patted against Lauren's fingers, making her giggle. "Wow, she was ready for that."

Bitsy took only five minutes to down the bottle.

"Goodness, should we give her some more?" Mom asked.

Lauren shook her head. "No, this is how much Mike said for now. The powder container tells how much to give during an entire day based on the size of the puppy, and then you have to divide that up between the feedings." She gave a big yawn, and on her knee, Bitsy did the same.

Mom laughed. "I think we should all go to bed. Especially if we have to be up at six thirty to feed her again."

Lauren looked up at her mom hopefully. "Mom, my bedroom is nice and warm, and if I have her box in there, I can keep an eye on her...."

"But we have to feed her so early. You don't want to get up at six thirty during vacation!" Dad smiled.

"I do, I really do!" Lauren promised. "I was the one who woke up and found her, Dad. I really want to help."

Dad looked over at Lauren's mom. "What do you think, Annie?"

Mom sighed. "I suppose so. But only for tonight, Lauren. Tomorrow, when she's a little stronger, Bitsy can go back with Baylee and the other puppies."

Lauren nodded eagerly and picked up the cardboard box. Inside, Bitsy was snuggling up against the well-wrapped hot-water bottle. Lauren thought she looked happier than she had all day. She padded back up the stairs, yawning uncontrollably. She set the box down next to her bed, and fell asleep listening to the tiny wheezy breaths from inside the box.

It was really hard to get up when Dad came in at six thirty, but Lauren dragged herself out of bed, and carried Bitsy's box downstairs to watch Dad prepare her next bottle. The trip downstairs hadn't disturbed Bitsy at all, she noticed with a smile. The puppy was still snoozing peacefully next to the cooling hot-water bottle.

In the kitchen, Baylee was out of the puppy pen looking hungry, and Lauren fed her while Dad boiled water in the kettle.

"Can I feed Bitsy again?" Lauren begged, and Dad handed her the bottle.

"You might as well—you certainly seemed to have the knack earlier!"

Going downstairs might not have woken Bitsy, but the smell of the puppy formula certainly did, and she was gasping and squeaking with excitement as soon as Lauren held the bottle to her mouth.

After she'd cleaned Bitsy up, Lauren took her over to Baylee. She and Dad hovered anxiously, not too close to the puppy pen, watching to see how Baylee would react.

"I hope Bitsy will be all right," Lauren muttered. "It said in that pamphlet that sometimes the mom tries to lick the human smell away and accidentally hurts the puppy."

Dad put an arm around her shoulders. "We'll watch really carefully," he promised. "And it's not as if Baylee's a dog at a big breeder's, who lives outside and doesn't really know people that well. She's part of our family. Hopefully our smell won't upset her too much."

"Look!" Lauren whispered.

Baylee was sniffing thoughtfully at Bitsy, and Lauren held her breath as Baylee started to lick the little puppy. But Baylee didn't look at all upset, just a little surprised.

Lauren giggled. "I think Baylee's so worn out that she hardly noticed Bitsy was gone!"

Over the next few days, Lauren was sure that Bitsy had started to recognize her. If Bitsy started squeaking in her box, she would calm down as soon as Lauren picked her up, but not if it was Mom or Dad. Lauren knew it was probably just that Bitsy recognized her by smell as the person who usually fed her, but it still made her feel special. She couldn't wait for Bitsy to open her eyes, so that the puppy could see her as well as smell her.

Mom and Dad were supposed to be taking turns doing the night feedings, but Lauren couldn't help waking up when she heard the alarm go off in their bedroom. And once she was awake, she just couldn't stay in bed. Mom even stopped saying anything about it by the end of their second night of puppy-rearing.

Bitsy was putting on weight now,

although not as fast as the other puppies, who were round and glossy-furred. She adored her feedings, but Lauren suspected she might always be a little smaller than her brothers and sisters.

Bitsy squeaked and sucked at Lauren's fingers as Lauren scooped her up. She knew Lauren's scent, and she was sure it was time for Lauren to feed her, and she was so, so hungry.

Lauren giggled as Bitsy's little pink paws flailed around. "I'm just waiting for it to cool down. You don't want to burn your mouth!"

Bitsy squeaked even louder. Where was the milk?

"Okay, okay, here you go."

Bitsy sighed happily, and settled down to sucking. That was much better.

After the first week, Lauren and her parents could leave Bitsy for six hours in the middle of the night without a feeding. Dad said he'd do the midnight feeding on his own—he was used to staying up late working anyway. Lauren had to admit that it was really nice to get a good night's sleep again, even though she still had to get up super-early for Bitsy's morning feeding.

Carolyn came to visit the puppies when they were about two weeks old.

"Can I feed Bitsy?" she asked hopefully. "That photo you sent me of you feeding her was so cute. She's even more beautiful now that her eyes are open, though."

"She is, isn't she?" Lauren agreed, handing Carolyn the bottle.

Bitsy watched Lauren the whole time she was feeding, and Lauren could tell she was confused why somebody else was holding her bottle.

"You have to burp her now, like your mom burps Amy," Lauren told Carolyn when Bitsy had finished.

Now that the puppies were two weeks old, their eyes were open, although they still hadn't really started to move around much. The really exciting thing was that their markings were starting to come through. Bitsy had more brown on her face now, not just her pretty eyebrows, and all the puppies were changing every day.

Even though the puppies were still too tiny to really play with, Carolyn didn't want to leave when her mom came to pick her up.

Lauren waved good-bye from the door and sighed as Carolyn's car disappeared down the street. She really missed seeing her best friend every day.

"Lauren, I've got some really exciting news," her mom began as she came back into the kitchen. "Hey, what's the matter?"

"I just wish I could see Carolyn more often during vacations, that's all. Emails and phone calls aren't the same as having a friend close by."

Her mom gave her a hug. "This is going to be extra-good news for you, then." She beamed at Lauren. "We've rented out the cottage. To a family with a boy the same age as you!"

Lauren blinked. The cottage was

on the other side of the orchard, just beyond the barnyard. The old tenant had left a long time ago, and Lauren had forgotten they were trying to find someone new.

"His name is Sam Martin, and he has a little sister named Susan. Isn't that wonderful? You'll have a friend really close by!"

Lauren nodded slowly, but she wasn't sure it was all that wonderful. What if she didn't like this boy? And even if she did, he wouldn't be as good a friend as Carolyn.

Chapter Five

"Oh, that sounds like the Martins at the door!" Mom bustled around the kitchen, putting the kettle of water on the stove. "Would you open it, Lauren?"

It was two weeks after Mom had shared the news about the new neighbors moving in, and they'd said they were going to stop by that afternoon. Lauren still couldn't help wishing it was a girl her age rather than a boy. And she didn't want some strange boy and his little sister messing around with Bitsy and upsetting her. Instead of opening the door, she quickly dashed upstairs with Bitsy, and stashed her in the box she'd slept in on the first night. Mom still let her take Bitsy upstairs occasionally, and Bitsy couldn't get out of the box yet, although she really liked trying.

Bitsy whined in surprise as Lauren put her down. What was happening? She had been enjoying a nice cuddle, and now she was being left all on her own! She stood up with her paws against the edge of the box, scratching hard. Where was Lauren? She whimpered miserably.

Lauren ran back downstairs and tried

to look friendly as Mom introduced her to Mrs. Martin and Sam, a blond-haired boy who looked just as embarrassed as she felt. Sam's dad was still sorting things out at the house, and his little sister was asleep, Mrs. Martin said.

Sam cuddled one of the puppies, the big boy that they had named Buster, and didn't really say much. Lauren was just hoping that they might go soon—surely they must have a lot of unpacking to do. But then her mom nudged her and said meaningfully, "Why don't you show Sam around the farm?"

Lauren frowned. It was almost time to feed Bitsy, and she didn't want to anyway!

Her mom glared at her, and she gave a

tiny sigh and turned to Sam. "Come on. You can bring Buster, if you like."

Sam nodded and followed her out into the yard. "He's really nice. Is he your favorite?"

Lauren shook her head.

"Don't you have a favorite? He'd be mine. He's great." Sam snuggled Buster up under his chin.

Lauren didn't know what to say.

It would sound silly to admit that she'd hidden Bitsy. "I like them all," she said, a bit vaguely.

Lauren trailed around the farm, showing Sam the orchard, and the old barn on the other side of the yard. There were a few bales of hay in it still, and she liked to hide in there sometimes.

"This is cool. I bet the puppies would love it in here," said Sam.

Lauren nodded. "They haven't been outside much yet, but Dad is making a wire run so they can play in the orchard."

Sam looked up. "Oh, that's my mom calling. I guess we have to go and unpack."

He handed Buster to Lauren, and they headed back to the farmhouse. Lauren supposed Sam was okay, really—at least he liked the puppies— but she didn't think they were going to be best friends or anything, which was obviously what Mom was hoping.

"He was nice, wasn't he?" Mom asked, as they waved good-bye to Sam and his mom. "Gosh, look at Buster!" She tickled the puppy under the chin. "He's huge. I need to put an ad in the local paper about new homes for the puppies. And there are a couple of good puppy websites, too."

Lauren swallowed. Her heart seemed to have suddenly jumped into her throat. New homes! She had almost forgotten about that—she had wanted to forget.

"But they're only a month old, Mom!" she cried.

"I know. But puppies go to their new owners at about eight weeks, and people don't just show up and take a puppy home. We'll have to let them come and see the puppies—and we need to meet them to make sure we like them." She hugged Lauren. "We're not going to give Baylee's beautiful puppies to just anyone, sweetheart, don't worry."

Lauren nodded. "But—but not

Bitsy?" she asked quickly. "She isn't big enough yet, Mom."

Mom nodded thoughtfully. "You're probably right. Bitsy will have to be a little older than the others when she goes. Not much though, I don't think. You've done so well feeding her; she's catching up to them." She looked at Lauren. "I know you really love Bitsy, and it'll be hard for you to say good-bye, but you'll still have Baylee, remember."

Lauren buried her nose in Buster's soft fur. She loved Baylee, of course she did. But Bitsy would have died if Lauren hadn't woken up that first night. It felt like she and Bitsy belonged together. But Lauren just didn't think she could explain that to Mom.

She put Buster back in the puppy pen and ran upstairs to get Bitsy. When she opened her bedroom door, Bitsy scratched at the side of the box with her claws, squeaking frantically.

"Oh, I'm sorry. I went off and left you, didn't I?" Lauren scooped up the puppy, her eyes filling with tears. "I didn't mean to." She sighed, feeling Bitsy wriggle and squirm against her neck. "I don't ever want to leave you. But I'm not going to, am I? You're going to leave me. Oh, Bitsy, I don't want you to go!"

Summer vacation went by so quickly! Lauren thought. She could hardly believe that there was less than a week to go until school started! She supposed it was because she'd been busy all the time taking care of Bitsy and Baylee, and the other puppies.

Bitsy's brothers and sisters loved the little outdoor run that Lauren's dad had made for them, and spent lots of time out there now. Lauren's mom had put a photo of them all bouncing around on the grass on the pet website where she was advertising them to new owners.

Lauren wasn't sure about letting Bitsy go out in the run yet—she was still so much smaller than the other puppies, and Lauren was worried that they might hurt her with their rough and tumble games.

"Mom, can I take Bitsy out to play in the orchard, if I'm really careful not to let her run off?"

Her mom put down the phone. "Yes, that's fine. Although I'm sure she'd be all right in the run with the others, you know. She's a lot bigger now."

Lauren sighed. She supposed Bitsy was catching up. But she still wouldn't feed from Baylec like they did. Dad said she liked her special bottles too much. They wouldn't have to do the bottle feedings for too much longer, though. Now that the puppies were five weeks old, they were all eating solid food, too. Lauren loved to watch them eat.

The first few meals had gone everywhere but into the puppies' mouths, and Baylee had ended up having most of it as she'd licked it off the puppies. They had the same dry food as Baylee, but mixed with the puppy milk Bitsy had, and they always ended up with mush caked all over their ears.

"Who was on the phone?" Lauren asked, as she finished her toast. "It wasn't someone about the puppies, was it?"

"No, it was just Nicky, Sam's mom. We'd talked about sharing the rides to and from school next week, and she wanted to know if we'd rather do morning or afternoon. I said we'd pick you up in the afternoon. Is that okay?

I like hearing about your day."

Lauren gaped at her. "Sam's going to my school?" she asked.

"Well, of course he is. Yours is the only school close by."

"He's not in my class, is he?"

"No, he's in the other class." Her mom frowned. "His mom and I talked about it when they came over. Didn't you hear us?"

Lauren shook her head. She supposed she'd been too busy being grumpy about having to entertain Sam. And now she had to share rides to school with him! She knew it would make less work for Mom and Dad, but she didn't want to share her car rides; she liked having the time to talk to them.

Angrily, she picked up Bitsy and a

ball from the puppy pen and stomped out into the yard.

Bitsy squirmed excitedly in Lauren's arms, sniffing all the interesting new smells. She'd been everywhere in the house with Lauren, but this was different. A butterfly fluttered past, and she yapped at it in delight. When they got to the orchard, which had a brick wall all around it, Lauren gently put her down on the grass.

Bitsy looked up at her, not sure what she was supposed to do. She gave an inquiring little whine.

"Go play!" Lauren rolled the ball, and Bitsy chased after it, yapping. She tried to sink her teeth into it, but it was just too big, and she ended up rolling over on top of the ball with a squeak of dismay.

Bitsy bounced up and went off sniffing around in the grass, until she came to a plant with huge leaves. She licked a leaf thoughtfully, and then seized it in her teeth, pulling hard. It sprang back, and she jumped around yapping fiercely, until Lauren nearly choked with laughter.

All of a sudden there was a heavy thud, and a soccer ball bounced over the orchard wall and thumped onto the grass right next to Bitsy, who whimpered in fright. She scampered over to Lauren.

Lauren snatched Bitsy up in one arm, grabbed the ball with the other, and ran across to the wall to find Sam peering over it.

"Hey! You almost hit Bitsy with that! What are you doing?" Lauren snapped.

"Sorry! I was just kicking the ball around…." Sam looked guilty.

"You could have hurt her!" Lauren told him as she shoved the ball into his hands.

"Sorry…," Sam muttered again, and he walked away with his shoulders hunched over.

Lauren almost felt sorry for yelling at him, but then Bitsy wriggled into her neck, whimpering, and Lauren felt angry all over again.

When school started the next week, Lauren had to share rides with Sam, as her mom had arranged, but Lauren hardly talked to him. She didn't really know what to say, and Sam seemed shy of her. She supposed it was because of the way she'd talked to him in the orchard.

It was great being back at school and seeing all her friends again, but she really missed Bitsy and the other puppies.

"Are they big enough for new homes yet?" Carolyn asked at recess.

"Mom has people coming to see them already, and they can leave Baylee after next week, she says. People have already chosen six of them. Not Bitsy, though; she's still too little." *Thank goodness*, she added silently. Over the weekend, a family had come to see the puppies, and the little girl had picked up Bitsy, saying she wanted her. Lauren had felt sick watching. Luckily, Mom had seen her horrified face, and explained that Bitsy was too little to go for a few more weeks. The family had chosen two girl puppies named Daisy and Dani instead. But afterward, Mom had sat down with Lauren and hugged her, and explained that she was going to have to let Bitsy go sometime.

"You'll really miss her, won't you?" Carolyn said, putting her arm through Lauren's, and Lauren nodded.

"Couldn't you ask your mom and dad if you can keep her?" Carolyn suggested.

"I wish I could," Lauren whispered. "They've always said we can't, that we already have Baylee. But I just can't bear to think of Bitsy belonging to someone else."

Chapter Six

Bitsy watched the strange boy cuddling Buster and wondered who he was. There were lots of other people in her kitchen, too, but they all seemed friendly. Everyone who had come to the house over the last two weeks had wanted to pet her and her brothers and sisters, and play with them. It was fun, but it was confusing, too. She had a feeling that this boy was going to take Buster away. He had been here before, and this time he had picked Buster up right away, and Buster had wagged his tail and yipped happily, the way Bitsy did when Lauren cuddled her.

If Buster went away with this boy, then she would be the only puppy left. Daisy and Dani had gone with a little girl the day before. The girl's mother had put them in a special box with a wire front, and Lauren had taken her out to see Daisy and Dani drive off in a car. Lauren had hugged her extra tight, and seemed really sad, although she'd cheered up and giggled when Bitsy licked her ear.

Bitsy missed rolling over and over with all the others, now that it was just

Buster and her. She still had Lauren to play with, of course, and that was her favorite thing. But was she going to go somewhere, too, like all her brothers and sisters? She didn't want to. She wanted to stay here with Lauren.

The boy snuggled Buster under his chin, and then turned to put him into a carrier like the one Daisy and Dani went away in. Bitsy watched them go out into the yard, and then she looked around the puppy run, with its rumpled blankets and scattered toys, and howled a big beagle howl.

"Oh! Did Buster go today?" Lauren asked in surprise when she got home from playing at Carolyn's house.

"Yes, there's only Bitsy left," her mom answered. "Did you have a good time?"

"Yes, it was great," Lauren replied, only half listening. She was looking at Bitsy curled up asleep on the fluffy bed at one side of the puppy run. She seemed so tiny and alone.

Bitsy woke up and stared around her at the empty run, looking confused. She let out a tiny whimper and staggered to her feet, sniffing around the pen. Baylee leaned over and licked her gently, and Bitsy stopped whimpering, but she still looked uncertain.

Mom put her arm around Lauren. "She's gotten so much bigger, hasn't she? And you can really see all the brown coming out on her now. She's going to be so beautiful. You did really well with the hand-rearing, Lauren; it was such hard work. Dad and I are very proud of you, you know."

"Thanks," Lauren muttered. She was proud of what she had done with Bitsy, too, but she had a horrible feeling that she knew what was coming next.

"I know you'll miss her, sweetheart, but she's ready to go to a new home," Mom said gently. "She's hardly bothering with her bottles, and she's eating dry food now."

Lauren nodded, and sniffed. It was all true, but that didn't make it any easier. She pulled away from her mom with a muttered "Sorry!," picked up Bitsy, who squeaked in surprise, and fled upstairs.

Lauren was really looking forward to Friday and the start of the weekend. She enjoyed being back at school, but she missed Bitsy so much—and she wasn't sure how much more time they had together.

Her dad had picked up Sam and her as usual, and they sat in the back seat while Dad tried to ask cheerful questions about how Sam was settling in, and Sam kept saying things like, "Okay," and "Fine, thanks."

They dropped Sam off, and then Lauren ran inside to say hello to Bitsy.

The phone was ringing as she went into the kitchen, and her mom yelled from upstairs, "Can you answer that, Lauren? I'm just making the beds!"

Lauren grabbed the phone, hoping it wasn't an order for her parents' camping supplies company, as she always worried she'd get them wrong.

"Hello?"

"Is this Mrs. Woods? With the beagle puppies?"

"Oh! Yes—I mean, I'm her daughter," Lauren explained.

"Oh, good. Do you have any puppies left? I just saw the website."

Lauren swallowed. This lady might end up being Bitsy's owner. All of a sudden her eyes filled with tears. "There is one puppy left," she said, making her voice sound very doubtful.

"Is there something wrong with it?" The lady on the phone sounded worried.

"Well…. She was the smallest of the litter, much smaller than the others. We had to hand-rear her."

"Oh, dear. Well, if she's not healthy I think I'll try someone else. Thanks anyway."

Lauren pressed the button to end the call with a shaky hand, and put down the phone.

But she couldn't answer the phone every time someone called….

Still feeling really guilty, Lauren took Bitsy out into the yard to play. She threw a ball for Bitsy to chase, and she raced up and down the yard with excited squeaks.

"Lauren!" Mom was calling from the small, grassy area next to the house where the clothesline was. "Can you help me hang the clothes, please?"

Lauren sighed. Hanging the clothes was one of the jobs she did to earn her allowance. "Sorry, Bitsy," she said, picking her up. "You go in the run, okay? I'll be back soon."

Bitsy stared after her, whining. Lauren had left the ball on the grass, and there were no toys in the run. Bitsy ran up and down, sniffing at the wire, then scratched at it, wondering if she could get out and fetch the ball. She stuck a small paw through the wire fence, but the ball was too far away to reach.

Yapping angrily, Bitsy scratched at the wire again, standing up on her hind paws. Her claws caught in the wire. She looked at them thoughtfully, and unhooked them. Then she stretched up higher, clinging on tight. She was climbing! Wriggling and scrambling, she worked her way up the side of the run. She teetered on the top, not quite sure what to do next. All at once, she let go and scrambled down the other side, landing in a little heap.

She sprang up and shook herself excitedly. There it was—her ball! She chased after it, pushing it along with her front paws, and followed the ball as it rolled through the front gate and out into the yard.

Ten minutes later, Lauren dashed back, eager to keep playing with Bitsy, only to find that Bitsy wasn't there.

She stood staring at the run. The fence was about two feet high—surely Bitsy was too small to climb out!

"Bitsy! Bitsy!" Lauren cried, as she ran all around the run.

But the little puppy was nowhere to be found.

Chapter Seven

Bitsy padded across the yard, and set off exploring around the other side of the orchard wall. She'd abandoned the ball in favor of all the other interesting things she could smell. Maybe she'd find Lauren if she went down here, too. She spotted a snail climbing up the wall and watched it round-eyed. She went closer and sniffed. It had an odd smell, and she decided it wasn't for eating.

"Hey! Bitsy!" Bitsy jumped, and looked up. That wasn't Lauren's voice.

It was the boy, Sam, holding a big ball. She'd seen him before when he came to the house to pick up Lauren in the mornings. She sniffed his fingers in a friendly sort of way. Maybe he would play with her….

"Are you supposed to be out here on your own?" he asked. "I bet you're not."

"Bitsy! Bitsy!" There was a distant voice calling, sounding worried.

"You're definitely not," Sam told Bitsy. "That sounds like Lauren looking for you."

Bitsy could hear Lauren, too, but she wasn't quite sure where she was. She whimpered anxiously.

"It's all right. Let's find Lauren, okay?" Sam looked down at her, and Bitsy pawed his foot eagerly.

"Come on. Good girl." Sam put the ball down and picked up Bitsy. He walked quickly toward the yard. "Hey, Lauren, I've got her!"

Lauren came dashing out of the front gate. She grabbed Bitsy, hugging her tightly while Bitsy whined with delight. "Oh, you're terrific, Sam! I was really worried. She must have climbed out of her run. Thanks!"

"Beagles are really good at escaping." Sam nodded, and Lauren looked at him in surprise. "I really like dogs," he explained. "We can't have one, because Dad is allergic, but I've got a ton of dog books. And I once saw a video on a website of a beagle climbing out of a huge pen."

"Oh." Lauren suddenly felt really ashamed. She'd been going to school with Sam every day, and she hadn't asked him anything about himself, or said a single friendly thing. "It's wonderful that you found her. What if she'd gone out into the road?"

Sam nodded. "I can't imagine losing a dog like that," he agreed. "It would be awful."

Lauren's eyes suddenly welled up.

"I'm sorry! I didn't mean to make you cry!" Sam said, looking horrified.

"It's okay," Lauren gulped. "It's just—you don't understand...." She wiped her hand across her eyes, while Bitsy licked at her cheek anxiously.

"Bitsy isn't mine. Not forever. She's going to have a new home, just like the other puppies. And I can't stand the thought of not having her anymore."

"Oh, wow," Sam muttered. "I thought you were keeping her, when she stayed and all the others went. And she's with you all the time."

"I've always known she'd have to go, like her brothers and sisters," Lauren whispered. "I still have Baylee, and of course I love her, but I've spent so much time with Bitsy, because we hand-reared her. It's going to be awful when she leaves. It was bad enough when people came for the others, but Bitsy is special." She opened the orchard gate, and gently shooed Bitsy in. "Want to come and play with her?" she said.

Sam nodded and followed her. "Has anyone come to see Bitsy?" he asked.

Lauren shook her head. "Someone called earlier, and I sort of mentioned how Bitsy was the smallest one of the litter and made this lady think she wasn't very healthy...."

She glanced at Sam, not sure what he'd think, but Sam looked impressed.

"I felt really guilty afterward," Lauren admitted. "And I can't keep turning people away."

Sam looked thoughtful. "There must be something you can do. I'll help you." He looked at Bitsy, who was destroying an apple that had fallen on the ground. "You can't lose her," he said firmly.

Lauren smiled. He sounded so certain that it made her feel a little bit better.

The next morning, Sam knocked on the kitchen door while Lauren was finishing her breakfast, and slipping cornflakes to Baylee and Bitsy, who were sitting on either side of her chair.

"Good morning, Mrs. Woods," he said politely to Lauren's mom. "I was just wondering if Lauren wanted to come out and play."

"I'm sure she does!" Lauren's mom said, looking delighted, and Lauren rolled her eyes at Sam, who tried not to laugh.

"I'm popular, then," he said quietly, as they went across the yard with Bitsy and Baylee on their leashes.

"Mom thinks it's really nice for me

to have a friend living close by." Lauren swallowed nervously. "I'm sorry I haven't been very friendly. I was a little angry when Mom arranged the rides and everything—like I didn't have a choice."

"Me, too!" Sam agreed. "My mom kept going on about how lucky I was, and I was like, she's a girl and I've never even met her! I'm sorry," he added. "Anyway, I've got a plan!"

"You do?" Lauren asked eagerly. "Tell me."

Sam sat down on the rusty old tractor that had been abandoned on the edge of the field and beamed. "I think we should buy Bitsy ourselves! I've got $30 of birthday money left. I'd give you that, no problem, if I could share Bitsy. Take her for walks sometimes and stuff. It's the closest I'll get to having a dog, after all."

Lauren nodded slowly. "I have the money my grandma gave me at the beginning of summer vacation, but I've been so busy with the puppies I never got around to spending it. That's $50 so far. Puppies can't cost more than $100, can they? But how are we going to get the rest of the money?"

Sam grinned. "I thought we could pick the apples from the orchard and sell them. We could set up a stand on that big patch of grass where the road down to the farm ends. It's close enough to the main road for people to see us and stop."

Lauren jumped off the tractor wheel. "That's a great plan! Mom and Dad never have time to pick them, so they won't mind. I'll go get some buckets."

It took a while to pick the apples, because a lot of them had holes from wasps getting to them, and those had to be thrown on the compost heap— but eventually they had three buckets of really nice-looking apples. When they went back home for lunch, Lauren grabbed a handful of freezer bags from the kitchen. Sam found an old folding table in the big shed at the back of the cottage, and he borrowed one of the boxes from the move to make into cardboard signs.

Then Lauren had another idea. "You start selling the apples. I just remembered something—Mom's always saying I should go through my old soft toys. We can sell those, too. Here, you take Bitsy.

I'm going to head back home and get them."

By the time she struggled down the road with a garbage bag full of stuffed bears and dogs, Sam was looking very pleased with himself. "I've already sold three bags!" He'd made the signs as well, and tied a couple onto the bushes on both sides of the road.

apples
50¢

"That's great! Can you please help me put the toys on the grass in front of the table? They'll make people stop and take a look."

"Bitsy and Baylee have been making people stop, too. They've had a lot of attention."

It turned out that the toys were almost more popular than the apples. Lauren even had to go back and find some more soft toys that she hadn't been planning to get rid of, but she didn't mind giving up her toy beanbag dogs if it meant she could keep her real one.

"How much money have we made?" Sam asked, as they packed up at dinnertime.

"Twenty dollars!" Lauren beamed.

"So that's $70 altogether. And there are a lot more apples we can pick. But I don't think I have any more old toys."

Lauren's mom and dad were so happy that she was playing with Sam that they didn't ask what they'd been doing all afternoon. And they didn't mind at all when she and Sam and the dogs disappeared again the next morning.

It was the middle of the morning, and they were doing very well, when a car pulled up by the stand.

"Would you like some apples?" Sam asked, sounding very professional, and the man smiled and dug around in his pockets for some change.

"Actually, I'm looking for Redhills Farm," he explained, as Lauren handed the apples through the car window.

"It's down there," Lauren pointed.

"Thanks. I came to look at a beagle puppy—is that the mom? She's beautiful." He nodded at Baylee, who was sitting by Lauren's side. He couldn't see Bitsy, as she was curled up asleep, half inside Sam's hoodie top.

"Y-yes…," Lauren stammered, and the man waved and drove away.

Sam and Lauren stared at each other in horror. The man had come for Bitsy! They were too late!

Chapter Eight

"What are we going to do?" Lauren whispered. "We can't let him have her. We really can't! Mom didn't say anyone was coming. He must have just showed up."

Sam nodded. "We almost have enough money, too. It's not fair."

Lauren looked at him, frowning. "If Bitsy's not there, he can't see if he likes her…," she suggested slowly.

"You mean we should just stay here?" Sam asked.

Lauren shook her head. "No. Because he's seen us, and Mom knows we have Bitsy. We have to hide. Come on!"

"Where are we going?" Sam asked.

"I don't know yet. Let's just get away from here."

"Okay." Sam zipped up his hoodie, and used it like a bag to carry Bitsy, while Lauren grabbed Baylee's leash.

Bitsy woke up as they ran back down the road, as Sam was jiggling her around inside his top. She gave an indignant squeak and tried to wriggle out.

Lauren turned back. "I'll take her. She'll be quieter with me. Shhh, Bitsy!" Bitsy snuggled gratefully into Lauren's arms as Sam handed her over.

As they peered around the corner of the barn, they saw the man's car parked in the yard. The top half of the back door was open and they could see him talking to Lauren's mom in the kitchen.

"Let's hide in the barn," Lauren said quickly. "If we go behind the bales of straw, we'll still be able to see if they come out."

They sneaked through the open doors, and settled themselves at the back of the barn.

"Shhh! I can hear my mom," Lauren whispered.

"Lauren! Lauren!" They could just see Lauren's mom, looking a little embarrassed. "She's probably in the orchard, playing with Bitsy," she said.

"I'm sorry. I should've called first," the man said. "I saw the ad and thought I'd just stop by, since I was coming this way. There were two children up at the top of the road with a beagle."

"Oh! Well, that would be Lauren and Sam. I hope they haven't gone along the road. Lauren knows not to. I'd better go up there and find them. You stay here and drink your tea."

Lauren sank back behind the straw bales. "She's going to be upset when she sees we aren't there," she said slowly.

"Do you want to let your mom know where we are?" Sam asked.

Lauren chewed her lip uncertainly, but then Bitsy woke up again inside Sam's hoodie and wriggled out. She gave a little yap, and looked up at Lauren with her big brown eyes. She looked so beautiful that Lauren knew she couldn't bear to let her go. "No," she said firmly. "He'll give up waiting soon, hopefully."

Bitsy climbed off Lauren's lap and went sniffing around the floor, and nudging up against Baylee, who was quietly curled up on a pile of straw. Baylee yawned and licked Bitsy half-heartedly. It looked like she just wanted to sleep.

Bitsy could smell delicious smells all

around the barn. She padded off around the edge of the bale to investigate, and Lauren and Sam both dived to grab her, which made Baylee bark.

"Shhh!" Lauren hissed, putting her finger to her lips, and Baylee gave her a confused look. "I'm sorry, Baylee, sweetie. But we have to be quiet, okay?"

Sam put Bitsy in his lap, and started to wave a piece of straw for her to chase. "I don't think we can keep this little one quiet, though," he said, as Bitsy squeaked delightedly and growled at the straw.

"They might not hear from out there. Oh, there's Mom. She looks worried," Lauren said guiltily.

Lauren's mom went into the house, and obviously told the man she couldn't find Lauren and Bitsy, because he came out and got into his car.

"I'm so sorry," Lauren's mom said.

Lauren thought the man looked disappointed, but she was more worried about the anxious look on her mom's face.

The man handed Lauren's mom a piece of paper. "Here's my phone number, anyway. If you could give me a call." Then he drove off down the road.

Bitsy growled at the straw again. Sam had stopped waving it around, and she was getting bored. She whined loudly, and tugged the hem of Lauren's jeans with her teeth. She wanted them to play properly.

"Should we come out, now that he's gone?" Sam asked.

Lauren wanted to, especially since she could hear her mom calling for her dad, who was working in the office at the back of the house. Now they'd both be searching for her. But she shook her head. "What if they just call the man to come back?" She nibbled her nails. "I think we have to wait a little longer."

They could hear Lauren's mom and dad going around the house shouting her name. Finally, Baylee started whining. "I know, Baylee," Lauren whispered. "I'm hungry, too."

"I'm starving," Sam muttered, and then he gasped as he heard a different voice. "That's my mom!"

Sam's mom came running into the yard carrying Susan. Susan was crying and calling, "Sam?"

Sam and Lauren exchanged a guilty glance.

"I'm sorry, but I have to go. Susan looks really upset...." Sam was getting to his feet. "You stay, and I'll say I wasn't with you."

"It's okay. I'm coming, too," Lauren told him. "And I promise you won't get into trouble. I'll say it was all my idea." They crept over to the barn door and peered out anxiously. Baylee looked around their legs, unsure what was going on. Only Bitsy was happy and squeaked excitedly to see everyone.

"Sam!"

"Lauren!"

"Didn't you hear us calling you? We've been shouting for a while!" Lauren's mom hugged her. "We had no idea where you were!"

Susan struggled down from her mom's arms and ran to hug Sam.

"Were you in the barn the whole time?" Dad asked, looking from Lauren to Sam and back again.

"Um, yes…," Lauren admitted.

"So you were hiding on purpose," Dad said.

Lauren glanced worriedly at Sam, and then said, very fast, "That man had come to buy Bitsy, and I didn't want him to."

Mom blinked. "He was very nice. He already has one beagle and wanted another. He was really disappointed when we couldn't find you."

"Sam, I can't believe you frightened us all like that," his mom said angrily.

"I think we'd all better go inside," Dad said firmly. "I want to understand what's going on here." He shooed Sam and Lauren and the two dogs into the kitchen, where Baylee and Bitsy went eagerly to their food bowls. "Sit down, you two. Now, explain. What was wrong with that man that made you decide to do something so silly? He seemed like he'd be a really good owner."

"Nothing…," Lauren began haltingly.

"It wasn't him," Sam put in. "We didn't want anyone to have Bitsy. Look." He dug in his hoodie pocket and brought out the old pencil case he'd been keeping the money in.

"Eighty-four dollars," Lauren said proudly as Sam emptied it onto the table.

Dad frowned. "I don't get it."

"We were going to buy Bitsy ourselves!" Lauren explained. "I really, really don't want to sell her to some stranger! We thought a puppy probably costs about $100, and we were so close to having it, and then that man came! We had to hide Bitsy in case he got her first!"

"Does this have something to do with the table full of apples at the top of the road?" Mom asked.

Lauren nodded. "We sold the apples from the orchard, and my old toys, too."

"And it's my birthday money."

"And my money from Grandma."

"There are more apples left," Sam added. "We should get to a hundred easily."

Mom smiled sadly. "That man was going to pay $400. That's what a pedigree puppy costs."

"Four hundred!" Lauren whispered in horror. "We couldn't raise that much. Oh, no...." And she started to cry. She was going to have to give up Bitsy after all.

Bitsy looked up from her bowl. What

was the matter with Lauren? She dashed across the kitchen floor and scratched frantically at Lauren's legs.

Lauren reached down and picked Bitsy up, cuddling her close, while Sam petted her head.

Bitsy howled loudly, joining in with Lauren's sobbing.

"Lauren, shhh…," her dad said gently. "And please tell Bitsy to hush, too. I can't hear myself think. That's better," he added, as Lauren petted Bitsy and shushed her. "We didn't realize you were that desperate to keep Bitsy. Why didn't you say something?"

"I tried!" Lauren burst out. "But you kept saying we had Baylee, and ever since the puppies came you'd said we couldn't keep them. I told Sam about it, didn't I?"

Sam nodded. "But we thought if we had enough money we could keep her. Lauren said I could share her, too."

"Oh, Sam…," his mom said sadly. "He loves dogs," she explained to Lauren's parents. "But his dad is allergic."

Lauren's mom was watching Bitsy, snuggling up in Lauren's arms, her eyes switching from person to person, as she tried to follow what was going on. "She is beautiful," Mom said slowly.

Lauren's dad looked at her. "It was you who said no more dogs, Annie!"

"Somehow I can't imagine being back to just one after all those puppies. It already seems very quiet, with only Baylee and Bitsy." Mom smiled. "And she's definitely the prettiest of the litter."

"So can we keep her?" Lauren asked,

not quite sure whether that was what her mom was saying. "Really? You mean it?"

Mom nodded, and laughed as Lauren hugged her, squishing Bitsy in between them. "Don't squash her!"

"But if Baylee has puppies again, we're not keeping any!" Dad said sternly.

Lauren shook her head. "Oh, no, I promise I wouldn't even ask!"

"You can have your birthday money back, Sam," Lauren's mom said, smiling.

Sam nodded, but he looked a little sad.

"Do you still want to share Bitsy, though?" Lauren asked, holding Bitsy out to him.

Sam nodded eagerly, and Bitsy wagged her tail so fast it almost blurred, and then licked his hand lovingly.

"We can use the apple money to buy her a really nice new collar and leash," Lauren suggested. "Not Baylee's old ones anymore. And we can put 'This dog belongs to Lauren and Sam' on her collar tag."

Everyone laughed, and Bitsy howled again, a real show-off howl with her ears thrown back and her tail wagging under Sam's arm.

Sam grinned. "I think she likes that idea."

HOLLY WEBB

Holly Webb started out as a children's book editor, and wrote her first series for the publisher she worked for. She has been writing ever since, with more than 100 books to her name. Holly lives in England with her husband, three young sons, and several cats who are always nosing around when she is trying to type on her laptop.

For more information about Holly Webb visit:

www.holly-webb.com
www.tigertalesbooks.com